The First Snowfall

Anne & Harlow Rockwell

MACMILLAN PUBLISHING COMPANY · NEW YORK

COLLIER MACMILLAN PUBLISHERS · LONDON

Macmillan Publishing Company
866 Third Avenue, New York, NY 10022
Collier Macmillan Canada, Inc.
Printed and bound by South China Printing Company, Hong Kong
First American Edition

10 9 8 7 6 5 4 3 2

The text of this book is set in 24 point Futura Book.
The illustrations are rendered in pencil and watercolor.
Library of Congress Cataloging-in-Publication Data
Rockwell, Anne F.
The first snowfall.
Summary: A child enjoys the special sights and
activities of a snow-covered world.
1. Snow—Juvenile literature.
[1. Snow] I. Rockwell, Harlow. II. Title.
QC929.S7R63   1987   86-23712
ISBN 0-02-777770-7

I saw the snow begin to fall.

Snow fell and fell
all through the cold and quiet night.

In the morning, I put on
red mittens, a plaid muffler,
my woolly cap, and warm boots

with my
new ski jacket
and pants.

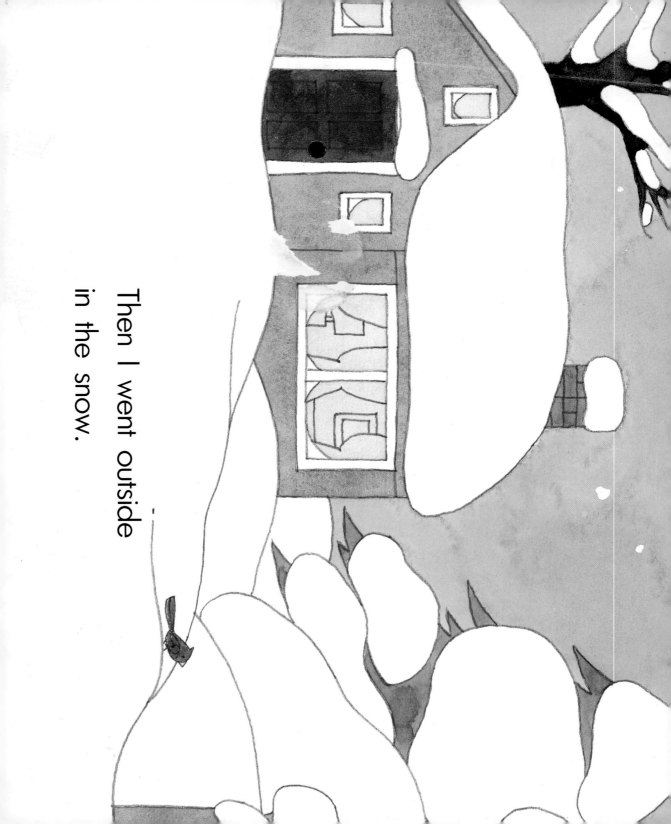

Then I went outside
in the snow.

I waved to the driver
of the snowplow
when it came down our street.

This is the snow shovel
I used

to shovel a path through the snow.

This is the snowball I rolled

to build our snowman.

Our car was covered with snow until we brushed it off.

This is the sled
we put in the car.

These are
my mother's
skis and poles.
We put
them in, too.

At the park,
I rode
on the sled
with my father.

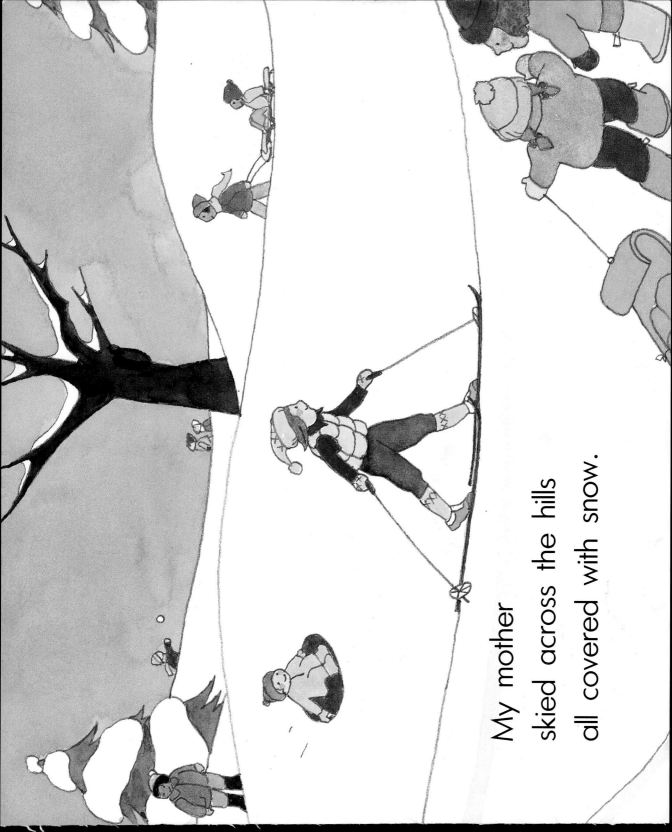

My mother
skied across the hills
all covered with snow.

This is the hot cocoa
I drank
when I came home.

It warmed me up.

Then I went outside
to play in the snow some more.